BROTHERS OF DESTRUCTION

BY TRACEY WEST

Grosset & Dunlap
An Imprint of Penguin Group (USA) Inc.

GROSSET & DUNLAP
Published by the Penguin Group
Penguin Group (USA) Inc., 375 Hudson Street, New York, New York 10014, USA
Penguin Group (Canada), 90 Eglinton Avenue East, Suite 700,
Toronto, Ontario M4P 2Y3, Canada
(a division of Pearson Penguin Canada Inc.)
Penguin Books Ltd., 80 Strand, London WC2R 0RL, England
Penguin Group Ireland, 25 St. Stephen's Green, Dublin 2, Ireland
(a division of Penguin Books Ltd.)
Penguin Group (Australia), 250 Camberwell Road, Camberwell, Victoria 3124, Australia
(a division of Pearson Australia Group Pty. Ltd.)
Penguin Books India Pvt. Ltd., 11 Community Centre, Panchsheel Park,
New Delhi—110 017, India
Penguin Group (NZ), 67 Apollo Drive, Rosedale, North Shore 0632, New Zealand
(a division of Pearson New Zealand Ltd.)
Penguin Books (South Africa) (Pty.) Ltd., 24 Sturdee Avenue,
Rosebank, Johannesburg 2196, South Africa

Penguin Books Ltd., Registered Offices: 80 Strand, London WC2R 0RL, England

ISBN 978-0-448-45584-6   10 9 8 7 6 5 4 3 2 1

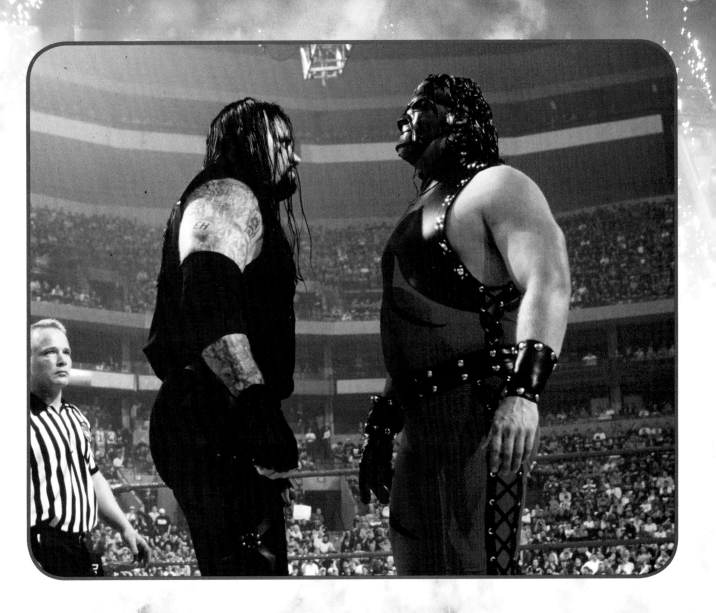

When two Superstars are inside the ring, anything can happen. Rivals battle rivals. Friends battle friends. And sometimes brothers battle brothers.

The rivalry between Undertaker and his brother, Kane, is legendary. When they attack each other, the results are devastating. But when they team up to become the Brothers of Destruction, their opponents shake with fear.

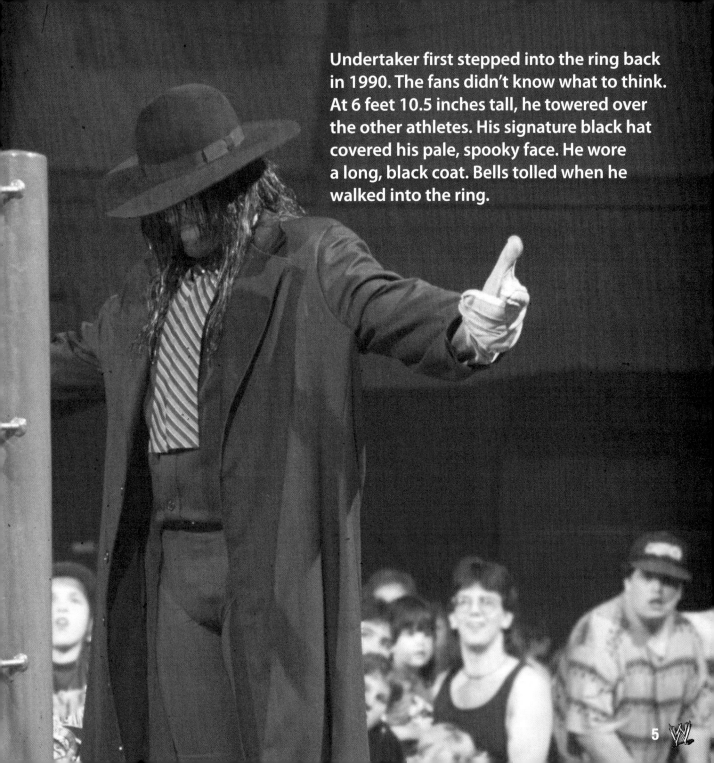

Undertaker first stepped into the ring back in 1990. The fans didn't know what to think. At 6 feet 10.5 inches tall, he towered over the other athletes. His signature black hat covered his pale, spooky face. He wore a long, black coat. Bells tolled when he walked into the ring.

The Deadman didn't say much, but he didn't need to. Few Superstars could match his skill and power. Some were too terrified to even face him. Undertaker liked to challenge his foes to a Casket Match. He won by stuffing his opponent into a coffin—and closing the lid!

One day, Undertaker's creepy manager, Paul Bearer, had some news for Undertaker. He said that Undertaker's long-lost half brother, Kane, was looking for him. Undertaker didn't know what to expect.

Soon all the fans were wondering when Kane would appear. They got their answer at Bad Blood in 1997, just in time for Halloween. Undertaker was battling Superstar Shawn Michaels in a steel cage. Suddenly another Superstar ran up to the cage. The mysterious newcomer was seven feet tall and wore a red top, red tights, and a red-and-black mask over his face.

It was Kane! He ripped off the steel door and ran inside the cage. He and Undertaker stared each other down. Then Kane attacked his brother with Undertaker's own move: the Tombstone Piledriver. Kane picked up his brother, held him upside down, and then dropped to his knees. *Slam!* Undertaker hit the mat. Kane left the cage, and Shawn Michaels pinned Undertaker for the victory.

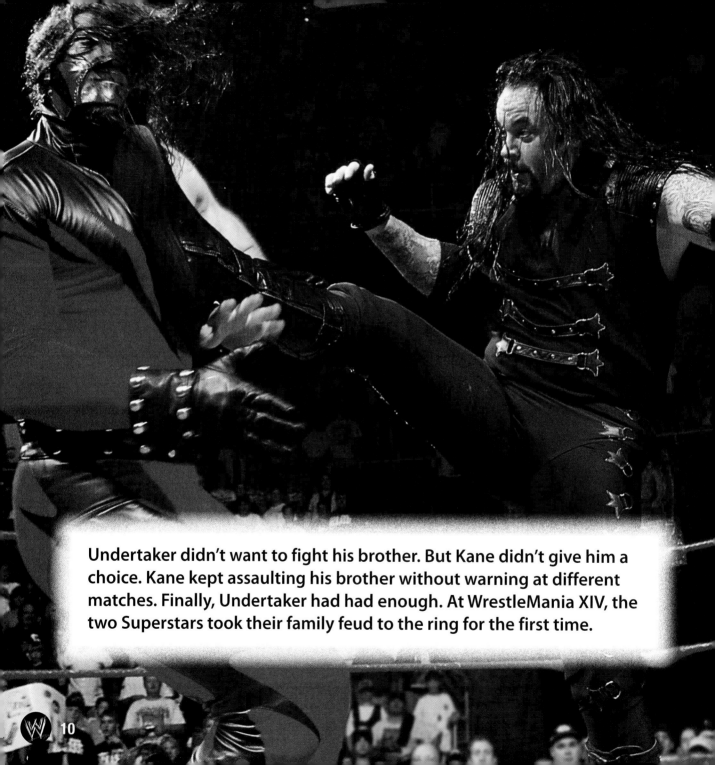

Undertaker didn't want to fight his brother. But Kane didn't give him a choice. Kane kept assaulting his brother without warning at different matches. Finally, Undertaker had had enough. At WrestleMania XIV, the two Superstars took their family feud to the ring for the first time.

Undertaker had never lost a WrestleMania match, and he wasn't about to start now. Kane Tombstoned his brother twice during the match, but Undertaker didn't stay down. He pounded the ring with Kane that night and won the match.

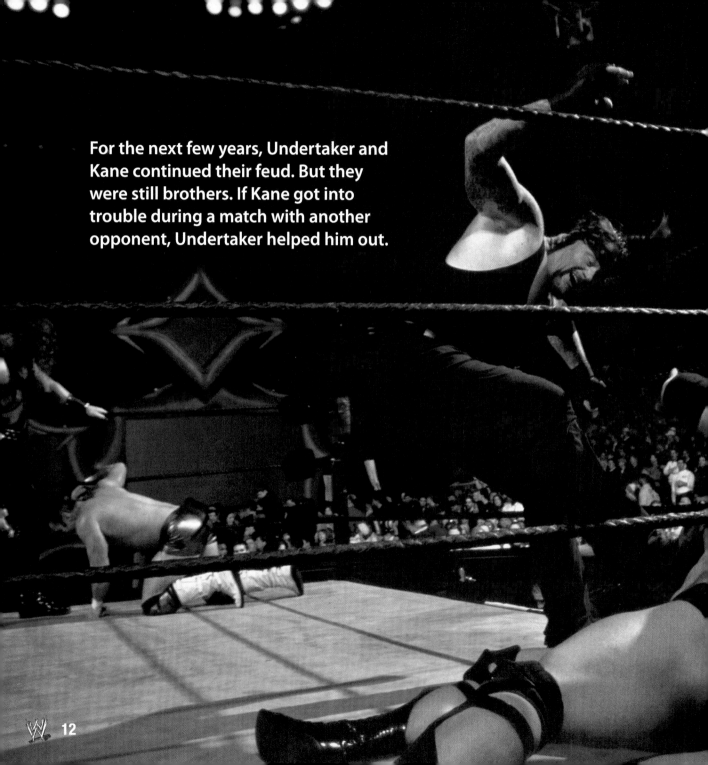

For the next few years, Undertaker and Kane continued their feud. But they were still brothers. If Kane got into trouble during a match with another opponent, Undertaker helped him out.

In 2001, the brothers teamed up for the first time at the Royal Rumble. In this thirty-man match, a new Superstar enters the ring every three minutes. Kane came in first and dominated, eliminating seven Superstars by himself before his brother even entered the ring. Then Kane and Undertaker worked together to take out the competition.

That was how the Brothers of Destruction were born! These two titans paired up to form a tag team. They fought their first match on *SmackDown* against Rikishi and Haku. The two powerful islanders couldn't withstand the twin towers of terror, and the Brothers of Destruction won their first tag team match.

Then the brothers set their sights on the WWE World Tag Team Championship. They battled two other teams at No Way Out in 2001. But Rikishi and Haku wanted revenge. They interfered, and the Brothers of Destruction lost the match.

The brothers got another chance for gold at *SmackDown* on April 19, 2001. It started when "Stone Cold" Steve Austin and Triple H assaulted Kane, injuring his arm. Undertaker couldn't help his brother—he was busy fighting Edge and Christian in the crowd. The angry brothers demanded a match against Edge and Christian that very night.

During the match, "Stone Cold" and Triple H attacked Kane once again. That left Undertaker to face Edge and Christian alone. He knocked out Edge. Then . . . *Bam!* He slammed Christian to the mat with a powerbomb. The Brothers of Destruction were the new World Tag Team Champions!

They didn't hold the championship for long. At Backlash, the brothers took on "Stone Cold" and Triple H in a title match. Kane's arm was still bandaged from the sneak attack. Undertaker did the best he could to protect his brother. But in the end "Stone Cold" and Triple H walked away with the World Tag Team Championship.

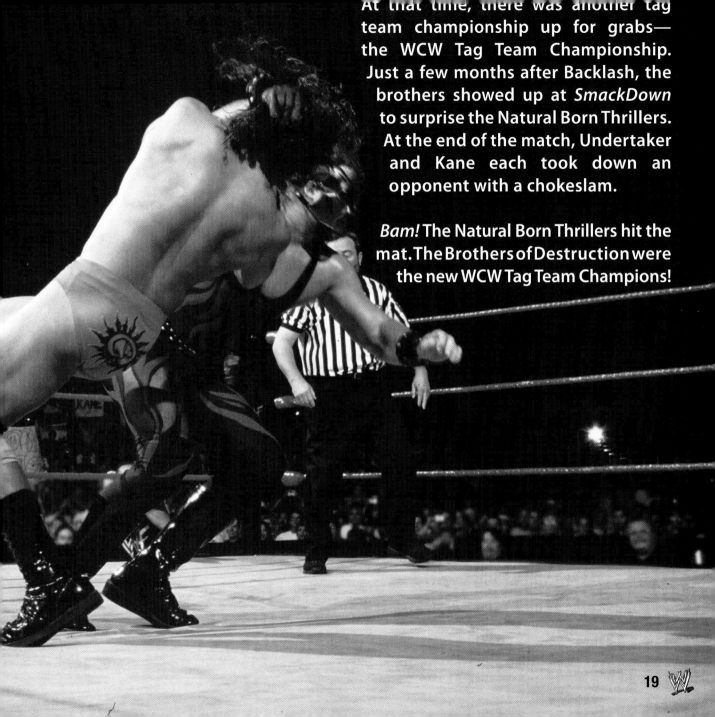

At that time, there was another tag team championship up for grabs— the WCW Tag Team Championship. Just a few months after Backlash, the brothers showed up at *SmackDown* to surprise the Natural Born Thrillers. At the end of the match, Undertaker and Kane each took down an opponent with a chokeslam.

Bam! The Natural Born Thrillers hit the mat. The Brothers of Destruction were the new WCW Tag Team Champions!

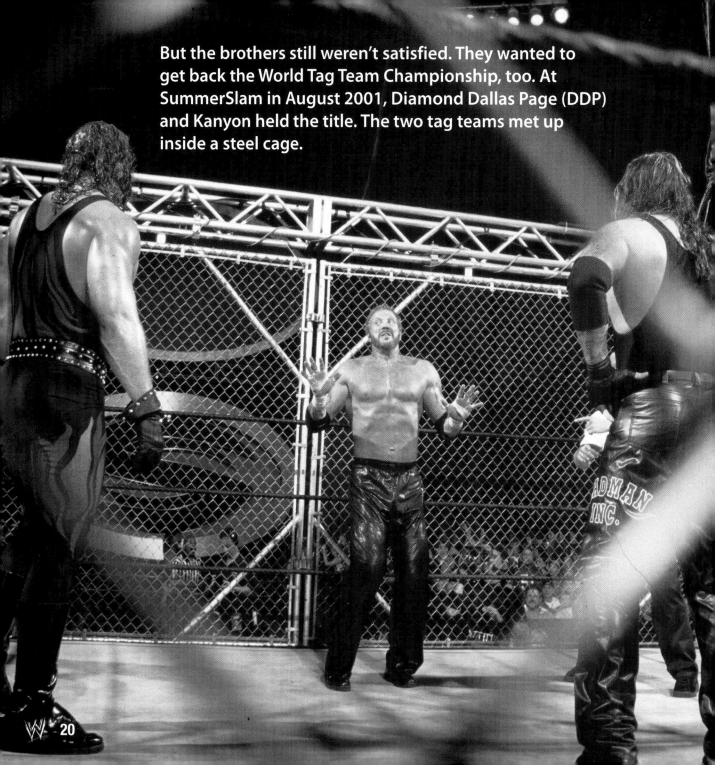

But the brothers still weren't satisfied. They wanted to get back the World Tag Team Championship, too. At SummerSlam in August 2001, Diamond Dallas Page (DDP) and Kanyon held the title. The two tag teams met up inside a steel cage.

Right from the start, DDP and Kanyon tried to climb the cage walls to escape the Brothers of Destruction. But Undertaker and Kane grabbed them, slamming them into the cage walls. The four Superstars traded blows in a grueling battle. In the end, Undertaker crushed DDP with his huge powerbomb, the Last Ride. Now the Brothers of Destruction held two tag team championships!

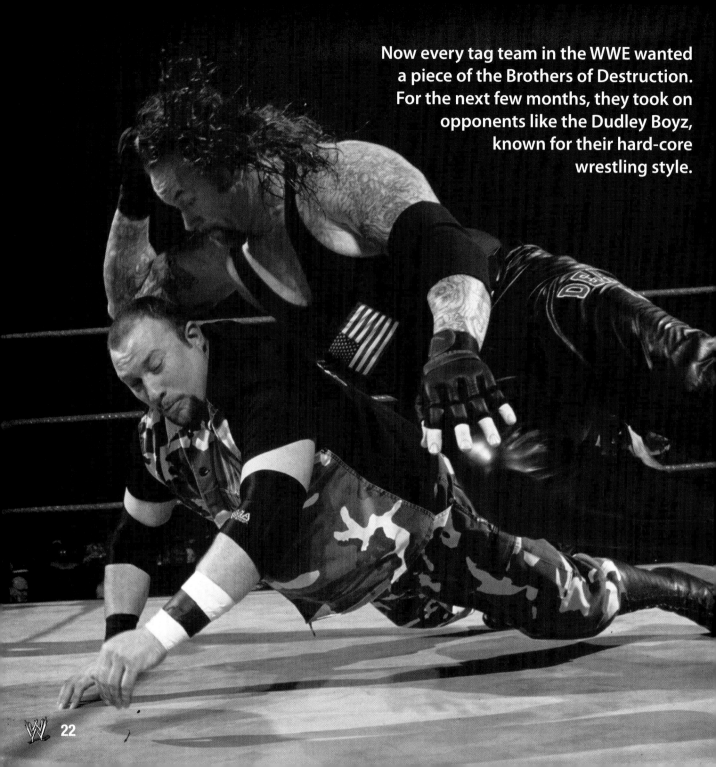

Now every tag team in the WWE wanted a piece of the Brothers of Destruction. For the next few months, they took on opponents like the Dudley Boyz, known for their hard-core wrestling style.

The Brothers of Destruction were at the top of their game. But old grudges soon broke the brothers apart once more. Undertaker and Kane went solo. Then, in a dramatic match, Triple H defeated Kane and the Big Red Monster was forced to take off his mask. For the first time, the world saw Kane's face. After that, Kane tore through the WWE like an angry hurricane.

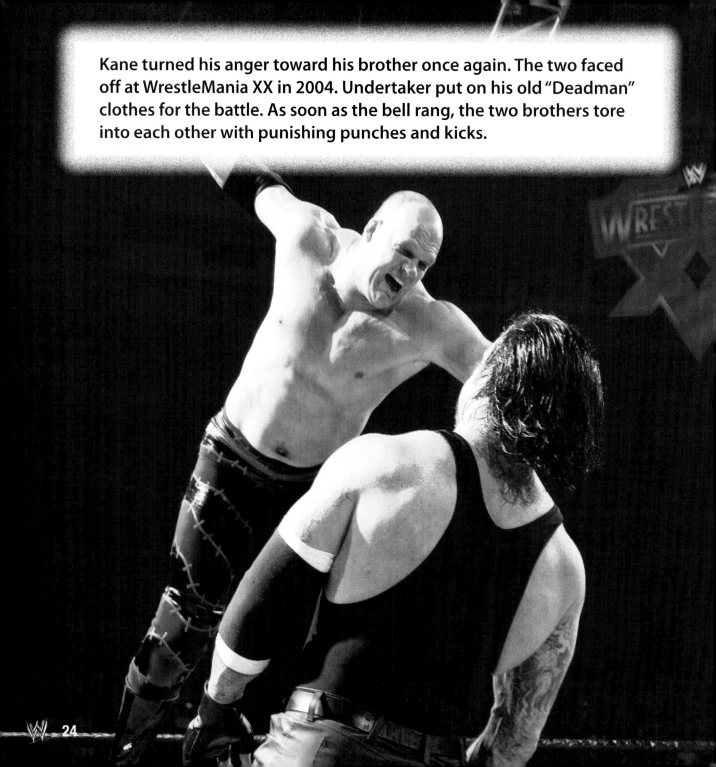

Kane turned his anger toward his brother once again. The two faced off at WrestleMania XX in 2004. Undertaker put on his old "Deadman" clothes for the battle. As soon as the bell rang, the two brothers tore into each other with punishing punches and kicks.

It was an old-school brawl, featuring plenty of clotheslines and chokeslams. It looked like the brothers were evenly matched. But after a powerful chokeslam sent Kane slamming into the canvas, Undertaker unleashed a Tombstone Piledriver. *Wham!* Kane hit the floor, and Undertaker pinned him. Match over!

It looked like the Brothers of Destruction might never get back together. But Undertaker has said that one of the few things that warms his dark heart is fighting alongside his brother, Kane. The tag team reunited several times over the next few years. They took on tag teams including MVP and Mr. Kennedy, King Booker and Finlay, and MVP and Matt Hardy.

The Brothers of Destruction dominated every time they got together. "It is amazing to see these two monsters together!" the ring announcer crowed. "It's like something out of a Steven Spielberg movie!"

Leading up to Backlash 2008, the Brothers of Destruction teamed with Triple H and John Cena to battle Randy Orton, JBL, Edge, and Chavo Guerrero. The match ended when Edge pinned Kane for the win—but the best action was still to come!

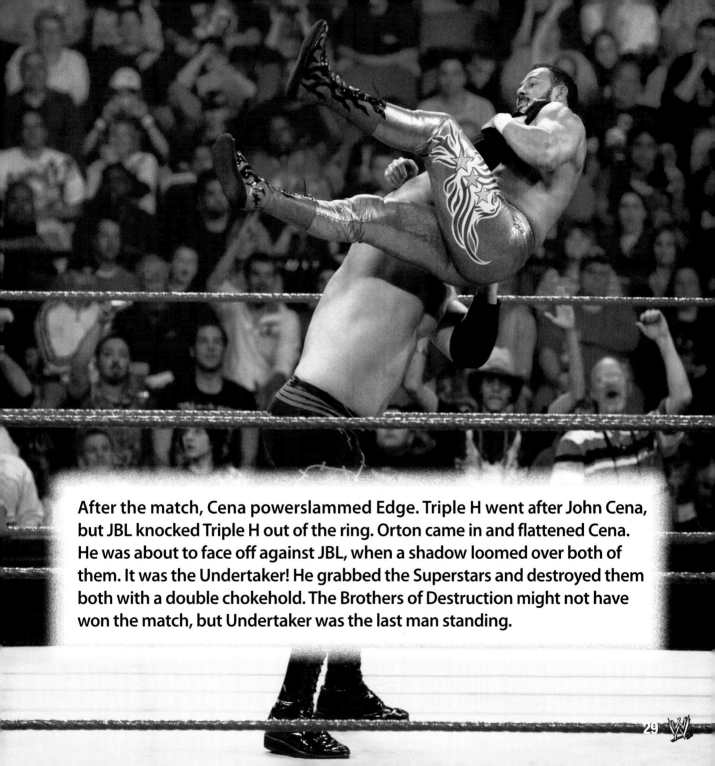

After the match, Cena powerslammed Edge. Triple H went after John Cena, but JBL knocked Triple H out of the ring. Orton came in and flattened Cena. He was about to face off against JBL, when a shadow loomed over both of them. It was the Undertaker! He grabbed the Superstars and destroyed them both with a double chokehold. The Brothers of Destruction might not have won the match, but Undertaker was the last man standing.

In 2009, the brothers faced one of their biggest challenges ever. At *SmackDown*, they competed against Chris Jericho and Big Show. At seven feet tall and nearly five hundred pounds, Big Show is one of the few Superstars the Undertaker can look up to. The match would be a real test of the brothers' abilities.

But the brothers didn't disappoint. They worked together to hoist Big Show right over the ropes! A terrified Chris Jericho ended the match when he stole Undertaker's World Heavyweight Championship belt and fled the ring in fear.

No one knows when the Brothers of Destruction will join forces once more. But blood is thicker than water. When the next challenge arises, Undertaker and Kane will rise to face it . . . and their opponents will tremble beneath their mighty shadows.

TEMPORARY TATTOO INSTRUCTIONS

TO APPLY:
1. Clean and dry your skin completely.
2. Carefully cut out the tattoo that you want to apply.
3. Remove the clear protective cover sheet.
4. Place the tattoo facedown on skin.
5. Wet the back of the tattoo with a wet cloth.
6. Apply pressure and wait 20 seconds (don't rush).
7. Peel off the paper backing.

Your tattoo can last for several days.

You may wash your tattoo lightly with soap and water.

TO REMOVE:
1. Saturate the tattoo with baby oil, cold cream, or household rubbing alcohol.
2. Wait 20 seconds. Rub it away with a cotton ball or tissue.

WARNING: DO NOT APPLY TO SENSITIVE SKIN OR NEAR THE EYES.

Tattoo Ingredients: FD&C Blue No. 1, FD&C Yellow No. 5, D&C Red No. 7, Carbon Black 7, Titanium Dioxide, Styrenated Acrylic Copolymer Emulsion, Siloxane Defoamer, Water, Alcohol*

Adhesive Ingredients: Compound Synthetic Resin Emulsion

* Volatile material, not expected to be present in the dry printed ink film

Published by Grosset & Dunlap, a division of Penguin Young Readers Group, 345 Hudson Street, New York, New York 10014. Printed in the U.S.A.

Ages 3 and up